3 1160 00217 6753

WITHDRAWN

D0463707

The First

TEDDY BEAR

The First
TEDDY BEAR

By Helen Kay

Illustrated by Susan Detwiler

Stemmer
House
PUBLISHERS, INC.

Owings Mills, Maryland

Text copyright © 1985 by Helen Kay
Illustrations copyright © 1985 by Susan Detwiler
All rights reserved

No part of this book may be used or reproduced in any form or in any manner whatsoever, electrical or mechanical, including xerography, microfilm, recording and photocopying, without written permission, except in the case of brief quotations in critical articles and reviews.

Inquiries should be directed to
Stemmer House Publishers, Inc.
2627 Caves Road
Owings Mills, Maryland 21117

A Barbara Holdridge book

Printed in Italy

First Edition

Library of Congress Cataloging in Publication Data

Kay, Helen, pseud.
  The first teddy bear.

  "A Barbara Holdridge book."
  Summary: Describes how the first Teddy Bear stuffed toy originated inspired by President Theodore Roosevelt's refusal to shoot a little bear during a hunt.
  1. Roosevelt, Theodore, 1858-1919—Views on bears—Juvenile literature. 2. Teddy bears—Juvenile literature.
[1. Teddy bears. 2. Roosevelt, Theodore, 1858-1919]
I. Detwiler, Susan, ill. II. Title.
E757.K26   1985   973.91'1   85-2706
ISBN 0-88045-042-8

The First
TEDDY BEAR

Once, there was a president of the United States named
Theodore Roosevelt. He lived in the White House on
Pennsylvania Avenue in Washington, D. C.   Here,
everyone called him "Mr. President." The people called
him "TR" for short, after the first letters of his name. Very
close friends called him "TEDDY." He did not like that
name.

There was another man who lived on Thompson Avenue in Brooklyn, N.Y. He was not famous at all — not yet. He owned a candy store, and sold lollypops and chocolate kisses. His name was Morris Michtom. Children called him "the candy store man." He liked that name.

Morris Michtom had a secret. At night, after the candy store was closed, he made toys. Sometimes his wife Rose made little rag dolls. Sometimes he made little plush ponies. He did not make little bears — as yet.

Neither "TR" in Washington, nor Morris in Brooklyn, dreamed that they would become fathers of the Teddy Bear. But this was before the "great bear hunt" of 1902.

Even as a young man, TR was known as a famous hunter.

He rode the wilderness trails of the west. He searched for the spotted wild cat and the great elk. He climbed the Rocky Mountains to find the grizzly bear.

But when he became president, he was too busy to hunt — until 1902.

That fall, a five-day bear hunt was organized. The hunters went into the wild and rough country between the states of Mississippi and Louisiana. No one seemed to agree as to just where Mississippi ended and Louisiana began. Both sides were claiming the same unbroken wilderness.

The president came to help decide on the state borders. There would be time enough between bear hunting, it was hoped.

Now the local bears were nothing like the great western grizzly bear. These bears were small, for bears — "hog bears," they said, for size.

In fact they were black bears. But black bears could be brown or brownish, and they all had brown noses. When the sun shone on the fur of the little bears, the color turned a rosy golden cinnamon — the color of cinnamon cookies. And oh, how they loved honey! They could climb a tree for a honeycomb, as fast as a squirrel!

All at once the whole country was following the bear hunt in the newspapers. For along with the president came the newspaper reporters.

They told the country about the great bear hunt.

Newsmen wrote: "The hunting party climbed the 'mountains' of Mississippi, or was it Louisiana?" Since the "mountains" were bluff hills, and the borders were in doubt, it was very hard to know.

Back in Brooklyn, Morris Michtom, the candy store man, could not wait to close the candy store at night. He brought in all the newspapers from the newspaper stand. He wanted to read all the news. He wanted to know all about the president's big bear hunt!

The first day, the hunters put on their hunting clothes.

The hunting horn was blown and the dog pack was off, with "Old Remus," the hound dog, in the lead. The dogs would find a bear, then chase it towards the president, where he could get his shot.

The dogs crawled over rocks. No bear hid behind boulders.

They sniffed the bases of trees. No bears were hiding in the branches. They crossed brooks. They crawled into caves. They found nothing — not even bear tracks. All morning, it was the same — no sight of bear.

Suddenly, there was a wild chase. The hounds had sniffed out a bear.

The president was ready to shoot. He aimed, but...that bear got away.

The press reported: "Bears Terribly Alarmed."

On the second day, Morris Michtom could almost hear the leaves crunch and crackle beneath the hunter's boots. It was November. It was cold in Brooklyn. But in Mississippi it was 76 degrees, and hot.

This day, the dogs flushed out a deer. No one fired a shot. The deer fled into the thicket.

The press reported: "The President Lost His Shot."

The third day was Sunday, a day of rest, of reading and much talking.

The fourth day of the hunt, it rained.

The hounds found a bear. But that bear gave them a nine-mile chase. He was captured on a farm, far away.

The press wrote: "Bear Eludes President."

There was one last chance for bear, on the fifth day.

Would the president get a bear?

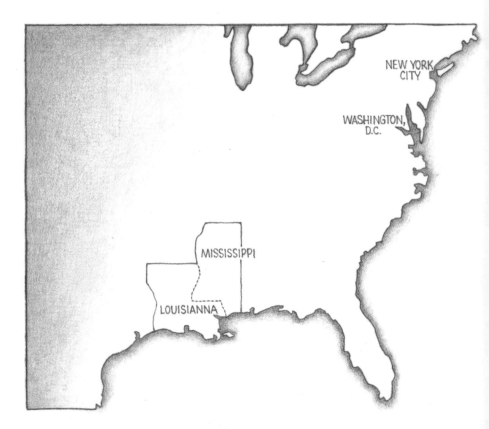

All over the country, the people were talking about the Mississippi bear hunt.

They hardly noticed that the boundaries between Mississippi and Louisiana were settled. Both states agreed to the borders. The president's work was done.

The morning of the fifth day of the hunt, the hounds picked up a bear track. The bears still avoided the president. The hounds could not chase a bear within range of the president's rifle. The hunters rode hard all day. But yet another bear ran away from the president's aim.

Then "Old Remus," the hound dog, just lay down and whined. He was too tired. The hunt master knew that this was the dog's last hunt. He blew the horn. The hunt was over.

Slowly the hunting party rode back to camp. Now there were no hunt dogs to flush for bear. But the president still had his gun at his side.

He rode through the tangle of brush. Then he came into an open sunny clearing near the camp, when there, directly before him, sat a small brown bear!

It's color was a rosy-golden cinnamon brown — the color of cinnamon cookies.

Squatting near a stump, the little bear was licking his paws. They were sticky with honey. The bear was not bothered by the bees that buzzed about his head. He did not even mind the president watching him lick his paws. The bear looked up at TR....

The whole hunting party was watching from a safe distance behind the trees. They looked at the bear. Then they looked at the president. They waited for the shot that would kill the bear. The president had the bear —right there — within his rifle range.

The bear did not move. It sat there, round as a toy. Its fur was golden, rosy in the sunlight...

The president raised his gun. Everyone waited for the shot.

But...he did NOT SHOOT. He lowered his gun.

The small bear scurried into the woods, still licking a paw.

"Why did you NOT shoot the bear?" the reporters asked.

The president said: "I do not shoot little baby bears."

The hunt was over. The camp broke up. The whole hunting party galloped the fifteen miles to their waiting train. It took them an hour of hard riding. The president was going back to Washington, the White House, and work.

While the train was rushing home, the newspapers carried the headlines: "President Ends Bear Hunt Without A Shot."

"Why," the reporters asked again, "didn't you shoot?"

The president replied: "I could not bring myself to shoot such a small sitting target."

DRAWING THE LINE IN MISSISSIPPI

The whole country laughed about the little bear that got away. There were chuckles and smiles all over the land.

The newspapers carried a cartoon called, "Drawing the Line in Mississippi." The president was holding up his hand to end the shoot. A little bear was being led away on a rope. Some papers reported that even the bears were laughing.

"Bears Laugh at the President," they wrote.

In the candy store in Brooklyn, Morris Michtom read the story in the newspapers and was happy all day.

That night, he decided to celebrate life. He set out to make a little bear, just like the one the president would NOT shoot.

Morris Michtom cut a piece of golden plush into a bear shape. He sewed on shoe buttons for eyes. His wife Rose embroidered a snout and a mouth. She stuffed the bear. They stitched on ears and arms and legs that moved.

When they were finished, Morris put the little bear in the candy store window. It sat on a hill of chocolate kisses.

Beneath the little bear was a card with its name: TEDDY BEAR.

People laughed with pleasure when they saw the new Teddy Bear toy in the candy store window.

However, the Teddy Bear did not stay there for long, because Morris Michtom was worried.

Perhaps a president would NOT like to have his name used for a toy? Perhaps some people would think that he did not respect the president?

Quickly he took the little bear out of the window. He packed it into an old candy box. He sent his newly made toy bear to the White House on Pennsylvania Avenue in Washington, D.C.

Morris Michtom asked President Theodore Roosevelt if he minded having a little toy bear named after him.

"Dear Mr. President," he wrote, "I do not wish to seem disrespectful, but I would like to call my toy TEDDY BEAR!"

No one knows what the president said when he opened the box. No one knows if he laughed very hard or long. But it is known that he was a very hearty laugher and he loved fun.

Yes, he kept that toy bear for himself and his children.

He sent a letter back to Morris Michtom in Brooklyn at the candy store.

The president said that the Teddy Bear now had a home with him and his children. The White House letter also said: The president cannot imagine what good his name would do, but Mr. Michtom was welcome to use it.

A late light burned in the candy store. Morris Michtom was making a new Teddy Bear for his store window. The next morning it sat in the store window. Along with the toy was the letter from the White House, giving permission for the name: TEDDY BEAR.

People came running to the store — but not for candy anymore. They came for Teddy Bears.

Morris Michtom became so busy sewing Teddy Bears that he had no time to sell candy anymore. Now he ordered bags of buttons and yards of golden plush cloth, instead of chocolate kisses and lollypops.

His wife Rose helped him cut out little bear bodies. Together, they sewed and stuffed. Orders for the Teddy Bear came from everywhere — even the biggest stores.

Finally, he closed the candy store. He called himself a toy company — the Ideal Toy Company.

Children in the country went to sleep at night cuddling their "Teddies," toy cubs, so round and chubby.

Children in the city snuggled their huggable Teddy Bears.

A "Good Night" song about the Teddy Bear was sung:
"Close your button eyes,
Let me smooth your hair,
Little Teddy Bear."

In the 1904 election for president, the Teddy Bear was on every campaign button. TR's daughter posed with a giant Teddy Bear.

The whole country was Teddy Bear mad. Even adults dressed up as Teddy Bears in stores and at ball games. So did the ball teams!

There were also Teddy Bear jokes.

"If "TR" is president with his clothes on," they asked, "What is he with his clothes off?"

The answer came back: "Teddy Bare."

33

Much later, the wife of the president's son, Kermit Roosevelt, wrote a letter to the Ideal Toy Company. She said that all the president's children and grandchildren loved the Teddy Bear. "I am placing the original Teddy Bear, which was sent to the president, in the Smithsonian Institution."

She felt she had to let them know. For the company's founder, Morris Michtom, had come to be known as the "Father of the Teddy Bear."

But in fact, the Teddy Bear had four fathers.

There was the president, "TR," called "Teddy" by his friends. He would not shoot a little bear.

There was the little bear himself, who walked into a clearing in the forest. He sat there licking his paws, golden, rosy in the sunlight, the color of cinnamon cookies.

There was the artist Clifford Berryman, of the Washington *Post,* who drew a small bear, the one that the president would not shoot.

And there was the candy-store man Morris Michtom, who made the first Teddy Bear toy with the help of his wife Rose, who did all the careful stitching.

Today, Teddy Bear sits in a glass case in Washington's Smithsonian Institution. Here it is seen and loved by children from all over the world, and by anyone, big or small, who ever owned a Teddy Bear.

ON CLIFFORD BERRYMAN

Clifford Berryman was the dean of cartoonists at the beginning of the century.

His first drawing on the Mississippi hunt was of a large bear. It appeared along with four other drawings on political events of the week in the Washington *Post*, Sunday, November 16, 1902. A second identical drawing appeared with a bear cub in other papers.

After the hunt, the little bear cub made a *Post* debut leading the whole hunting party out of the woods. But a few days later Berryman returned the little bear to his forest. He is found sitting in a tree: "So he would not land in the White House."

But land in the White House he did.

The bear cub evolved as a symbol of President Theodore Roosevelt. In fact, a Clifford Berryman button was made showing the bear cub carrying a banner saying: "I Am It," for the 1904 campaign. He also made little bear placecards for the famous Teddy Bear dinner in the White House.

In a personal interview with President Theodore Roosevelt, Clifford Berryman quoted the President as saying: "If I shot that little fellow, I could not look my boys in the face again."

President Roosevelt, though a great hunter, would not shoot any small animal which could not defend itself.

The same little bear was to appear in many Berryman cartoons. The bear cub appeared whenever Roosevelt was the subject, and later with Uncle Sam.

In Berryman's 63 years as a cartoonist, he made 15,000 political cartoons, working up to his 80th year.

When he heard that the TEDDY BEAR toys, inspired by his bear cub drawings, were being produced without credit, he said: "It gave the children pleasure. That is reward enough."

 ## MORRIS MICHTOM

Success with the Teddy Bear led Morris Michtom to found the Ideal Toy Company, which in time became one of the largest toy companies in America. Eventually, it was sold by the founder's grandson to the Columbia Broadcasting Company. By that time, Morris Michtom's company had produced millions of Teddy Bears for children all over the world.

Designed by Barbara Holdridge

Text composed in Times Roman, with Baskerville and Murray Hill display faces, by Brown Composition, Inc., Baltimore, Maryland

Printed on acid-free matte paper and bound by New Interlitho, S.P.A., Milan, Italy